I0553204

Sarah's Sensual Awakening

Dorian Shellan

Published by Haines Communications, 2024.

SARAH'S SENSUAL AWAKENING

First edition. February 18, 2024.

Copyright © 2024 Dorian Shellan.

ISBN: 978-1637860410

Written by Dorian Shellan.

Table of Contents

Sarah's Sensual Awakening

by Dorian Shellan

Chapter One: Sarah and Anna

Sarah had always lived in an old country house in Shropshire near the border of Wales with her father, mother, and an old faithful servant, Martha. Martha had been Sarah's mother's maid before she married her father, and was quite a confidential member of the family. Other servants rarely stayed longer than a year or so because the location was in such a quiet spot that there were no other people around. After all, what woman, other than an elderly one, could be expected to like a place where available men were so sadly wanting? For the twenty-four year old Sarah, though, life here had always been so even and tranquil that she never contemplated leaving it.

Sarah's father was a great reader of books, much versed in science, and his delight and her pleasure was her being taught by him. Botany, geology, animal and insect nature formed the chief and most interesting portion of their studies; but history, geography, French and Italian also found their place. Sarah learned to play the piano from her mother, and altogether, even without society, her education did her as much credit as if she had the advantages of a city maiden's life. For her whole life she had been content and happy. But all this was about to come to an end.

One morning in the early summer, Sarah's mother came down to breakfast without her father. She said she supposed that a long walk he had taken the previous day must have tired him, and that he was so sound asleep she had not the heart to waken him.

They ate breakfast as usual, taking care to make as little clatter as possible with the knives, forks, cups and spoons, lest any little clink might reach the ears of the sleeper above and waken him from a sound and refreshing sleep. After breakfast, Sarah went out into the garden to see what new flowers had blossomed, when she heard her mother shrieking out for Martha. She flew back into the house to see what was amiss while her mother called still louder for Martha, who came running as fast as she was able. As soon as they entered the bedroom, Sarah's mother pointed to her father. "I don't know what is the matter with him, but I cannot wake him."

Martha gazed earnestly into his face. He was dead. "He must have died very early this morning," she said. "For he is now quite cold and stiff."

The agony of the discovery was unbearable for Sarah's mother. She sank into a chair, gasped once or twice, and before anyone could run to her help she fell dead onto the floor, literally heart-broken.

Mr. Withers, Sarah's father's business associate advised her to think of some relative that she might ask to come and stay awhile, until some plan for the future could be made. "That might help to divert unhappy thoughts into some brighter channel," he suggested. "Ideally you would be able to go elsewhere for some time, but there is work for the lawyers, and much to be done before affairs can be put into good order. And whilst all this is being done your presence will be necessary."

There was only one suitable relative who came to mind, one of whom Sarah's mother had invited to make short stays with them several years back. "I know you didn't care too much for her back then," Martha told her. "But you're both older now, and she will be understanding about what it feels like to lose your parents."

Martha was right, Sarah did not care much for her. She was a town girl, with ideas and pursuits which were altogether different, and she remembered being offended with her for sneering at her "beetle and pebble hunting" occupations, which to her were tiresome and uninteresting. Still, it was the name of Anna Quinlan that first came into Sarah's head, so it was to her that Mr. Withers wrote.

Anna had also lost her parents a few years before and, like Sarah, she was an only child. Considering the previous friction between them, Sarah thought that Anna would never care to come, and actually hoped that she would not. Sarah was caught up in such a morbid frame of mind that it seemed unbearable for her to have to speak to others. The only person she cared to see was Martha, although even Martha had begun to scold her for not trying to bear up better.

But Anna did come. Having spent almost two years without a break in creating and setting up The Nunnery, the opportunity for a holiday in the countryside struck her as most appealing. Since Natalie Smithers, a recent addition to The Nunnery's ladies of pleasure, had also presented with capable organizational skills, Anna had employed her as house assistant and was, therefore, in a position to feel comfortable about taking time away from London. Almost as soon as she read the letter she packed up a trunk and left for Sarah's house.

Having not seen each other since they were girls, immediately upon arriving Anna was struck at what a beauty her cousin had blossomed into as a woman. Sarah stood tall, significantly above middle height for women. She had a lovely, slim figure, with beautiful hands and a naturally small waist. Her face was exquisite, with hazel eyes and the most perfect nose, mouth and teeth, all accented by the most lovely dark hair which cascaded down to her shoulders. In spite of her outward appearance, however, her demeanor was subdued and tearful, for Sarah could not hide the sad loss she had sustained by the deaths of her parents. But it was impossible for her to remain in the depths of desolation after Anna's arrival. Anna was new, and Anna was more her age, being only a couple of years older. And, having sustained the loss of her own parents at a similar age, Anna did not merely sympathize but actually provided true understanding and support.

At first all their conversations were of their parents, with Anna showing the greatest tact in gently leading Sarah's thoughts from the grave to the world around them, and its multiplicity of pleasures and delights. She insisted on taking good long walks in the countryside, where it was impossible not to feel the effects of fresh air and the songs of the birds. With exercise, Sarah returned to a more elastic state of health, and as her body improved in health so did her mind. Anna in old times had sneered at beetles, and weeds, and stones, calling the results of Sarah's natural history rambles all rubbish, but now she appeared to take delight in Sarah's teaching her about these things. Anna, quick and intelligent, actually seemed anxious to learn, that Sarah soon found herself growing excited in her eagerness to teach. If she referred to her dead parents it would be merely to tell Anna what they had said about these matters, no longer to rail and lament as she had first done. Weeks quickly passed away in this manner.

One day, while they were sitting beside the brook, Anna asked, "Sarah, do you intend to live here all your life?"

"Well," she answered. "I suppose so. After all, where should I go? And why would I not stay here?"

"Oh," Anna replied. "Without meaning to be at all rude to you, I do not think I could live here much longer."

"Oh, Anna!" Sarah was aghast. "You are not thinking, I hope, of going away yet? What should I do without you?" Her eyes welled up.

"There, there," Anna said, putting her arm round her cousin's waist and kissing her cheek. "I would not have said that if I had had any idea it would have made you cry. What I meant was, this is such a lonely spot. You never see a soul here from morning to night. I declare I have been here nearly a month, and except for old Withers, I have not seen a single gentleman inside the house. Are there no families with young men living near enough to have discovered the lovely Sarah, who hides her beauteous charms in these secluded groves?"

"Now Anna, please don't make fun of me. I may live in a very secluded spot, but I don't see why you should find fault with people for not taking notice of such an insignificant girl as myself."

"But Sarah, you are not insignificant. You are perfectly lovely, if you only knew it." Anna raised her hand to quiet Sarah's anticipated objections. "No, let me speak. If you saw more people you could not help noticing, if no one happened to tell you, that you are beautiful. Yes, beautiful. Your eyes are something perfect, and so is your face. You have lips which no man could resist longing to kiss. You have a lovely figure and a perfect bust, which I can see plainly through your dress that the high, hideous, stiff stays you wear cover two most charming little globes."

"Oh goodness, Anna, how you do run on. Do you think I care a straw what men may think of me? As for my stays, my mother bought them for me, and I think she was a good enough judge of what I required."

"Perhaps when you were just a girl. But you should now get others, like mine for instance, which give all necessary support without preventing the rounded globes being seen. It is really a shame to spoil a bosom like yours. A woman ought to take care of charms which have so powerful an influence over the imaginations of men."

"To what end?"

"Why, to see you in society, all dressed so as to show off all your lovely points to advantage."

"But suppose I don't care for society, and never wish to go into it?"

"Oh, but Sarah, you are talking of what you know nothing about. Being in society means great admiration, and who is there who does not like to be admired?"

"Well, I don't care about it for one!"

"Sarah, you are but a child and nothing else, in spite of all your science and stuff. You have been so buried here, that unknown to yourself, you have grown up in complete ignorance that there is a world of men and women about you, and that someday, perhaps not far off from now, you will have to take your place in that world. When you do you will, I venture to say, very soon find out what a charm there is in being admired.' She smiled. "But, as I asked you before, are there no young men in these parts?"

"No, Anna. I don't believe there are. We lived so very quietly that I suppose if there are any such creatures they never found us out. Our parish is quite a small one, and, as you may have seen in church, there are very few people in it, and no gentry. Papa used to be called 'The Squire.' "

"And you actually contemplate, without horror, the idea of living here by yourself for the rest of your life?"

"Oh no! I hope you will come sometimes and see me, Anna. Besides, I have old Martha, and I have my birds, and beasts, and flowers in the summertime. And my piano and my books in the winter. You have no idea of how very busy I am usually."

"But Martha won't be always with you. Of course I would be glad to come and stay with you sometimes. But only for short visits, for I would soon mope to death living here where I would see no one of the opposite sex."

"My goodness, Anna. How you do care about men."

"I am serious. As much as I care for you. I do not think I could live here much longer without being tired of myself, and even of you. Women require men just as much as men require women. If you had some handsome, agreeable young squires down here it would be pleasant enough to spend the days flirting in the fields and woods with them, but there is not a soul."

"Well, I declare I should not mind it I never saw another in my life!" Sarah made a quick nod and folded her arms

"That is because you have never known a town, my dear Sarah. You have never known what is to be wooed. You don't know the pleasure of courtship. You don't know what it is to have a man worship the very ground you have walked on."

"I really do not understand a word of what you are talking, about, Anna. To me a man is nothing, and as for love, except the love of my parents, or of dear old Martha, I know nothing. You mean something, I am sure, of which I have never heard. Of course a husband loves his wife, a parent his child, but I can't see what there is in such love for anybody to rave about as you do."

"Have you never read any novels, nor any love stories, Sarah?" Anna asked.

"Not at all. My father and mother said they were foolish stuff."

"I have heard others say so. But have you not even Sir Walter Scott or Shakespeare in the house?"

"Shakespeare we have, I know. But it is locked up in papa's study, in the glass bookcase. I have never read it."

"Ah, then read 'Romeo and Juliet' and you may perhaps learn a secret or two. I am particularly fond of 'Hamlet.'"

"The secret of love? But what is this curious secret, Anna?"

"Well now, Sarah, answer me. You are female, are you not?"

"Yes; of course I am."

"Of course you are. But why 'of course'?'"

"Because I am, I suppose. I was born so. I don't know of any other reason."

"Well! But there is a very good reason, if you only knew it. Why should you be formed different to a man, for instance? Can you tell me that?"

"I don't know, but what difference is there?"

Anna stared at her with very open eyes. "Oh, come Sarah. You don't mean to pretend that you have lived so long without knowing that there are most marked differences between a man and a woman?" She reached out her hand, and lightly placed it onto Sarah's lap. "Are you not immensely different from a man, right here?"

"Of course I am." She responded indignantly while shifting to one side to dislodge Anna's hand. "And I am well aware that a man is not formed there as I am. You are speaking of sex, Anna. And yes, I dare say that from my studies I know more about such matters than you." She laid back on the bank and looked up at the sky.

"You only know about sex academically, Sarah. But that is all." Anna lay on her side and smiled down at her cousin. "I, however, know all there is about sexuality." She stroked back the flop of hair that had fallen across Sarah's face, tenderly pushing it behind her ear before running her fingers down the side of Sarah's neck. "And sensuality. There is so much more for you to learn, Sarah. Let me teach you about sensuality, and then all that I have tried to tell you about the world will become clear to you."

"What do you mean by sensuality?"

"Have you never wondered why the female sex organ should be formed as intricately as you know it to be?" Anna asked.

"No. Indeed I have not given it any thought." Sarah's head drifted from side to side as she responded.

"If this were purely for the depositing of semen," Anna pressed her hand between Sarah's thighs. "Then wouldn't a simple hole suffice, instead of all of these sensitive parts?"

"Oh Anna, please don't do that."

"Why not? You are a girl and I am another. Surely one girl may touch another there? What harm is there in it?" Pressing her hand between Sarah's thighs, Anna gently stroked with her fingers.

"I don't know whether there is any harm, but oh!"

"What's the matter?" Anna asked coyly, a slight smile appearing on her face as she further pushed and moved her fingers about between Sarah's thighs

"My dear Anna, for goodness sake take away your hand. You are tickling me dreadfully." Sarah feigned a protest while st the same time easing her legs apart and making no move to disrupt her cousin's attentions. "If you go on like this you will make me scream."

"Scream away," Anna responded, laughing. "You may spend your breath, if you like, that way. But I mean to make you spend something else before I have done." She held Sarah tight with one arm and half lay on top of her, laughing and looking into her eyes.

The pleasure Sarah was now feeling was so intense, while at the same time seeming so shameful, that between the two feelings she was too distracted to even try to tear herself away. Very soon the tickling reached such a point that she felt, that if she did not find some way of relieving herself, she would faint.

Anna understood her cousin's plight perfectly. "Ah, if your dress were not so thick, and if you had not on two petticoats," she said. "I would have delivered you to orgasm before this." She leaned over and whispered into Sarah's ear, "But I don't think it is far off all the same."

As she spoke, Sarah felt herself jump under Anna's hand. Suddenly a thrill, a throb, shot through all that region, providing a delicious sense of some pent up flood bursting the ever lightening bonds which had held it back. "Oh, my," she gurgled. "So nice."

Anna took her hand away and threw herself completely on top of Sarah, enthusiastically holding down her arms and kissing her with the most passionate affection. "Ah!" she said. "So Sarah is sensitive to pleasure after all. I knew that a girl made like you must be."

"Please do get off me, Anna," Sarah gasped as she recovered. "I am nearly choking, and your weight is perhaps heavier than you think."

Anna planted one last kiss on Sarah's lips and rolled off to the side.

"Ah, now I can breathe." Sarah began to relax, then realized, "Oh goodness! I am all wet!"

Anna burst into a fit of laughter. "Of course you are, for I have made you spend. But imagine, if I had been a man and had been slithering into you instead of first tickling you with my hand, I would have made you spend a dozen times."

"I don't know what you mean."

"That is just because your thoughts have never rightly turned to such pleasure. I see now that you are as ignorant and as innocent as I thought you were only pretending to be. I have a great deal to each you, Sarah. And I will teach you, too." Anna began to rise. "But it is getting time for us to be going back, and I dare say you would like to put on some dry drawers."

Although initially pretending to be of the same mind, no sooner had Anna started to stand than Sarah pushed her over and made a grab at her. She turned Anna onto her back, putting her hand between her thighs, and began to treat her as she had been treated.

Instead of struggling, Anna lay perfectly still, and looking up into Sarah's glowing face asked, "what are you up to now, Sarah?"

"I am going to punish you and treat you the same way you treated me. Let's see how you like being tickled nearly to death."

"Oh?" Anna provoked her. "I defy you to tickle me. You don't know how to do it."

"Perhaps not as well as you do, but I will try anyway."

Anna had not nearly so thick a material in her dress as Sarah had, and she had on the lightest of petticoats and shift. Sarah felt the soft yielding charm under her moving fingers. Caressing the mound beneath the fabric, she traced the deep line which bifurcated it.

Anna lay quite quiet for the first minute, then suddenly gave a little start.

"Aha Anna. I can't tickle you, can I?" Sarah proclaimed triumphantly while she continued her movements, causing Anna's color to begin to rise and her bosom to heave. But then, curiously, Sarah began to feel a fresh tickling herself, though there was no hand in her lap. And the caressing of Anna's mound began to truly fascinate her.

All of a sudden, Anna clasped her cousin around the waist. "You have got on to it," she gasped. "Yes, keep your fingers moving just there. Oh, ah, that's it! Oh, Sarah! Ah! Ah I Oh my God! Oh how heavenly! A little quicker. Ah now, quick, quickly! Harder, ah-h-h there!"

Anna's increasing excitement excited Sarah even more. Whether it was sympathetic or not she didn't know, but as Anna screamed into climax she felt herself also spend again. She sunk on to Anna's bosom for a moment, and they both lay quite still.

At last Sarah raised her head and looked at Anna. Her face was flushed, but she had her eyes closed, and her lips slightly parted, and looked so still that Sarah thought she had fainted. Alarmed she shook her gently. "Anna, Anna," she said softly.

"What is it?" Anna answered languidly, "Oh, my, what exquisite pleasure you just gave me."

Reassured by hearing her speak, Sarah recovered and jokingly asked her, "well, now. Did I not tickle you?"

"That you did. And right well too."

"But you defied me to be able to do so."

Anna laughed. "Oh dear, I must have spent a cup full for I am drenched!"

"And so am I," Sarah admitted. "For I spent, as you call it, again, when I was finishing you off."

"That is most telling, Sarah." Anna pursed her lips and nodded as she rose to her feet. "That you were excited by dominating another gives me great insight into your true, underlying nature."

Chapter Two: Sensual Awakening

On returning to the house, Sarah immediately went to her room to change her drawers. When she went back downstairs she found Martha talking in a most animated manner to Anna. So animated that it was clear that Martha had been having a good glass or two. "Ah here the darling comes," she said, as Sarah entered the room. "We were just saying, Miss Sarah, that you are old enough, and big enough, to be showing your beauties to the world. For what's the good of a girl made like you hiding herself in the woods. You should be thinking of a handsome young lover. I dare say." The talkative old lady winked at Anna. "I'm sure Miss Sarah thinks so in her dreams."

"Not she," said Anna. "I've never known such a girl, Martha. I don't believe she ever thinks of a lover at all, and neither does she dream of one. Beetles, and butterflies, and old bits of stone are more her way."

"Ah well," replied Martha. "Miss Sarah may have a butterfly yet for a lover, and I'll be bound she will find he has a good pair of stones with him."

Anna burst into laughter. "And she will like feeling and examining them too. Eh, Martha?"

"In course she will, the darling. But look at the pretty innocent. She don't know from Adam what we are talking about."

"Well, I don't," Sarah blurted out. "And what is more, I don't want to. I detest the idea of lovers, and should never have thought of such a creature, but for Anna's chat."

"Ah well, dearie," said Martha. "Believe me, woman's comfort lies in man, so is a woman wanting until she has her man, to fit like into her."

Anna clapped her hands. "That is it exactly," she agreed. "Just like one of your beloved flowers, Sarah. Think of when the male part fits exactly into the female."

"I really do not begin to understand you." Sarah was bewildered, as well as now growing annoyed.

"Oh," Martha replied. "Miss Anna can explain all to you, Miss Sarah dear. I dare say most girls of your age would know it too, even without going to bed with a man."

"The idea!" Sarah objected.

"Seriously, dearie. You'll never know what pleasure means until you've been with a man."

Martha left the room to go about her chores and Sarah turned to Anna, exasperated. "Really, Anna, you must tell me all about men, and teach me. I feel like a fool when you and Martha go on so. I don't understand one atom."

"I'll happily tell you all," Anna promised. "But not here. I don't want to chat on matters it would be difficult to drop if that old lady were to suddenly come back in." She grinned. "I will tell you this, though. Contrary to what you have been led to believe through all your nature books, the drive for sex is not about the need to procreate. It is primarily driven by the pursuit of pleasure. Pleasure like what you experienced this afternoon."

Agreeably to her promise Anna joined Sarah in her bedroom that evening. "First, I want you to try on my stays," Anna began.

"For positively you must leave off wearing such barbarous ones as yours. So now, off with your dress and petticoats." So saying, she commenced to undo her own dress, and before Sarah had hers half unhooked she was in just her chemise and drawers. "There," she exclaimed, standing in front of Sarah. "Do you see how free my breasts are? They don't require support, for they are as firm as rocks, and hard as marble. Feel them."

Sara did as Anna bid her. She was immensely moved at the sight of the glowing bosom before her, so white and so beautiful. She reached out her hand, first on one and then on the other of the exquisite globes, and felt a great pleasure as she caressed them. Though not literally 'hard as marble,' they were decidedly extremely firm and elastic, and their shapes were perfect.

"Kiss them," Anna instructed.

Sarah did so with pleasure. It seemed to her as though some new revelation were opening up, for she never imagined there could have been anything so delightful in a girl's bosom.

"Now, quickly get off with that dress, you old slow coach," she teased. "Here, let me help you." In a moment she had Sarah in the same state as herself.

Sarah saw at once the hideousness of her stays, which were much too high, and much too rigid, and which fitted neither breast, waist, nor hips. Anna quickly had them unlaced, and opening the top of her chemise, which she complained of as being too high in the neck, slipped it off so that it fell to the ground. Except for her drawers, Sarah was now naked before her.

"Oh, the little beauties!" Anna exclaimed. "How nice, how firm. Why Sarah, I declare I should never have thought you had such perfections," she continued, pressing them in her hand alternately, causing Sarah's pussy to feel all tingly again. "What lovely, lovely, little rosebuds. Like tiny coral marbles, topping little mountains of snow. I must kiss and nibble them."

Down went her lips first on to one, and then on to the other, whilst her hand slid inside Sarah's drawers to take possession of her throbbing cunt. With the palm of her hand she pressed the rising cushion above the deep line, while her middle finger slipped in up to its knuckle and was completely buried into her rapidly moistening cunt. "What a sweet, sweet little cunt," she whispered. "How velvety and soft inside, and how quickly it responds to my touch. "

She rambled on, moving her finger up and down, occasionally withdrawing it to seek another spot, between the labia lips, near the top, and then pushing it in deep again, in and out, until Sarah felt ready to collapse from the pleasure. Anna then felt a convulsive little throb, which told her that Sarah was very nearly there. She clasped her, breast against breast, swerving her body a little from side to side so that their breasts rubbed backwards and forwards together. Then, lips open, she pressed against Sarah's mouth, who delighted in the feeling of Anna's moist tongue darting in and out between her teeth. Sarah was all on fire, and suddenly, with almost a pang of voluptuousness, she spent all over Anna's hand and wrist.

Keeping her finger still gently moving, Anna drew back her head. "Now, Sarah." She smiled. "Was not that a nice one?"

"Indeed it was," Sarah confirmed, feeling almost unable to speak from excess of emotion.

"Well, a man would give you fifty times as much pleasure with his hand, and a thousand times more with his prick. Oh, why am I not a man now that I might enjoy all these beauties?"

"I almost wish you were," Sarah replied, laughing. "For I am becoming most curious to know what new bliss there can be in store for me. But really, I believe you are making me lose every particle of modesty I ever possessed."

Anna laughed with her. "Modesty is the shift which covers the cunts of all women. It is a useful garment enough when we go abroad into society, and one which no wise woman would care to be without, but in intimate friendship, like ours, it becomes useless. I would not offend against modesty in public, but with you, or my lovers, I think it is a thing to be put off, and I like to be a natural woman on such occasions, quite naked. So let us strip all together now, and have a good look at the shapes nature has given us." She unbuttoned her drawers and let them fall to the ground, whisked off her garters, pulled off her stockings, and suddenly Anna was as naked as she was born.

Sarah was slow to follow, so Anna added her nimble assistance until Sarah was also in a state of perfect nature. But then a kind of shame took possession of her. She had never been naked in front of another, and instinctively put one hand over her mound while with the other hand and arm she attempted to hide her bosom, blushing under the keen gaze of Anna's beaming eyes.

"Oh, the charming, charming Venus de Medici," Anna cried, clapping her hands. "Don't stir from that position, Sarah dear; you are lovely, lovely. I want to walk round, and observe and admire you from all points of view. Don't stir. Just lift your hand a little bit off your cunt. That's it. Ah, I can see in you now what Venus was not permitted by her sculptor to show."

Anna chattered on, walking round and round and putting Sarah into various attitudes, and exclaiming, in what sounded language of exaggeration, at all the perfect beauties she saw.

During this time Sarah took equal stock of Anna and of her beauty, only half listening to her ravings being as absorbed as she was in gazing upon her.

"I feel that I am beginning to understand the sensuality you speak of Anna," she said. "So now you have the opportunity, tell me all about a man, and what it is he does to one."

"I shall sleep with you to-night," Anna responded while kissing her. "And we will have such a night of it. I'll tell you all you want to know, and I will show you even more."

Chapter Three: Lesbian Orientation

Anna and Sarah proceeded into the bed, where Anna immediately clasped her cousin in her arms, kissing her repeatedly. "Oh, Sarah," she said. "Lie back and I shall put my hand between your legs. Ah, that is it. Now I'll just slip my finger in this delicious little cunt of yours, like this, while you do the same to me. Am I not nice and hot, and soft inside?"

"Indeed you are, Anna, like velvet warmed before the fire."

"And so are you. But now we won't have any tickling yet. Now I will tell you about men."

"Ah do. I am dying with curiosity, Anna."

"When a man thinks of a girl and wants to have her, up goes his prick. It lifts itself with pride and power, and becomes just like a bar of iron covered from end to end with a thick, soft, velvety skin. If you were to take a good hold of one in that condition you could move your hand up and down, without the skin slipping from under your fingers."

"Really? How curious."

"Yes. Well, there it stands. And it has the most curious-looking head imaginable. It is something like a cherry at the end. This head is shaped there like a bell. It is blueish purple round the lower rim, which rim forms a regular shoulder. You can slip the movable skin right off the head, and behind the shoulder, and there it will stay, unless it is forcibly put back again.

Underneath the nose, as I will take it, of the prick, the movable skin is fastened, not far behind the point, and when the stand or stiffness is gone out of the prick this fastening pulls the cap over its head again."

"How very curious, and how convenient."

"Now under the prick, nearly as far back, but not quite, as the place where it springs from, is a very wrinkled bag, in which the balls are. I dearly love feeling a man's balls, and does not he like it, too? They feel slippery and hard, but you must take care not to squeeze them tight, as it hurts a man very much; but gently handling them, lifting them up with the tips of the fingers, and gently rolling them about in their bag, is most pleasing to every man, and if his prick has gone down, such treatment will quickly bring it back grand, and stiff, and big, and ready for work again."

"But the actual cause of its standing is desire?"

"That is correct. A man is able to give extraordinary pleasure to a woman with it, and I ought to know, for I have had plenty of experience. You know from your books that a penis inserts into a vaginal opening for intercourse, but your books cannot convey the delights enjoyed when he does so. That is what you must experience. Oh, if I only were a man. If only instead of this cunt I had a rattling, fine, big, long prick, as stiff as a poker, and a well-furnished pair of balls hanging to it, I would show you. I would show you what a real, good, unmistakable fuck is, for I am just the one who knows how it should be done, to be well done."

"Even though you are not so endowed, can you not tell me all the same? I am dying to know."

"Ah, my sweet Sarah is growing randy," she said, her voice growing thick and hurried, as though emotion were choking her.

"I will show you how a man gets onto you, and how he moves, and I will make you spend a dozen times, for I must either spend myself or burst!"

Anna positioned herself between Sarah's legs. "Open your thighs wide," she told Sarah in a most excited manner. "Open your thighs and draw up your knees. That is it." She sank onto Sarah's belly, put one hand under her hips to raise them, and the other she put round her neck. She pressed their bushy mounds together until the top of her cunt touched the bottom of Sarah's, then with pressing upward and downward sweeps thrilled her through and through with extraordinary and untold pleasure. Anna's grasp grew tighter, her breathing became more and more hurried, and then suddenly, when she had come to the end of one of her long upward sweeps, Sarah felt a warm, wet gush as Anna spent.

Immensely excited, Sarah clasped onto Anna and, rolling on top of her, took charge of the proceedings. She felt wild. Furiously rubbing her cunt against Anna's while kissing her face. They both spent again and again, until at length drenched, breathless, and tired, Sarah lay heavily on top of her cousin.

For a moment they were motionless, but then, lifting her head, Sarah asked, "That is how you do it with a man?"

"Something like that, yes," Anna responded with a hint of surprise in her voice. "But you seem to gravitate to being the controlling partner, which is generally the male role."

"Does the male experience as great a pleasure?"

"More than likely his pleasure is even more intense. So much so that he will actively seek it out." Anna rolled onto her right side to face Sarah. "But now that we have had some temporary relief, I'll do my best to describe what a man should do to give you the acme of pleasure. First of all he should put his prick into your hand. It is a most thrilling thing to feel, absolutely delightful, and you should feel it from end to end. Its hardness like iron, its soft velvety skin, its soft head, and its shifting hood. And then his grand balls in their wrinkled silky, soft bag, and the thick rough bush out of which this galaxy of manly charms grows. All form objects of delight to the hand that knows how to caress them, and to the cunt which expects so soon to feel their powerful action.

Whilst your hand is enjoying itself and giving your lover the greatest delight also, his hand will be stirring up the very depths of pleasure in you. By the way, before I forget it, let me warn you, when handling a man's prick in this way, do not caress its head too much. It is excessively sensitive, and too much rubbing produces spasms, very delicious for him but destructive of your pleasure, for you might make it too excited, and cause him to be too ready to spend. The longer a man takes during the fuck the greater your pleasure, for he does not spend over and over again during a fuck, but once only. That done he is done, too, for the time. So confine your caresses to the shaft of his prick, to his balls, his groins, and his bush, but leave the head of his prick alone, if you are wise."

"What will he be doing while I am touching him?"

"While you caress him so, he'll be kissing you, toying with your tongue with the tip of his, and he will also squeeze your dear little breasts. Presently his mouth will kiss you along your neck, until it reaches your bosom. He will kiss your breast with rapture, and nibble each little hard rosebud."

"And giving me absolutely wonderful sensations," Sarah giggled. "As you have shown me."

"Then, while sending you wild in this manner, his hand will glide over your smooth body and seek your mound. You will feel his hand press between your thighs, and he will stroke your cunt." Anna slid her hand to Sarah's pussy. "Like this. He will gently press the lips of your cunt together, and tickle your clitoris. Then he will slip his middle finger deep into your cunt, and tickle you there." She slipped hers in and found the narrow, tight, inner entrance.

Sarah gasped. Anna's touch made her feel on fire and she immediately, involuntarily spent.

"You quick little darling!" Anna exclaimed. "How you do spend. You are just going to love being fucked. But now," she continued, "You can feel, even from my poor little feminine hand, how very sensitive your cunt is all about the entrance. It is sensitive all along its whole depth, but the sensitive portion par excellence is about the entrance. The difference between a good fucker and an indifferent one, is in the fact that the really good fucker knows this. A man like that does his best to produce the most ecstatic pleasure in you by cultivating this extra sensitiveness of the entrance to your cunt." She kissed the side of Sarah's neck, then ran her tongue down to her left breast and sucked the erect nipple. "Would you like me to show you how he would do this?" She teased.

"Please..." Sarah moaned.

"Lie flat down on your back, across the bed, that's right, and part your legs."

Sarah did so, and Anna fell to admiring the inside of her thighs, kissing them as her wanton eyes wandered to regions higher still.

"Now Sarah, put one leg over each of my shoulders. Ah, that is it. Now I have this sweet little cunt of yours in full view. Lie still, so I might examine it to my entire satisfaction, as a man would wish to."

Sarah felt Anna's arms encircle her thighs. Her hands approached her bush, which she stroked, and then her fingers separated and parted the hairs which crossed the soft entrance to her cunt. These delicate little touches provided infinite pleasure, especially when she felt her press her thumbs gently so as to open the top of her cunt.

"Oh, such a sweet, little ruby clitoris," she cried. "Oh, Sarah, any man who lays eyes here must be compelled to kiss it." Then, down went her hot lips onto Sarah's cunt.

Sarah immediately cried out, "Ah, Anna. Don't do that. It is not nice." Despite enjoying the sensation, for she made no attempt to push Anna's head away, she feigned her objection because she felt a shock of modesty and inappropriateness to such an action.

"Not nice?" Anna raised her head. "Do you mean that I hurt you? That my kisses there are unpleasant to you?"

"No. On the contrary," Sarah gasped. "But surely it is not a nice thing to put one's lips on such a part of the body as that?"

"But I like to do it to you, and I like it done to myself, and I strongly suspect when you have had a little more of it you will like it extremely. Just see if you don't!" Her lascivious mouth sank onto Sarah's cunt again.

Since Anna said she liked doing it, Sarah found herself able to relax. She lay still, but only for a moment. Anna took Sarah's clitoris between her lips and began to mouth it, touching it smartly with her tongue in so ravishing a manner that Sarah could not help squirming with the excessive pleasure she was experiencing. She did not resist, but could not lie still. She moved under Anna's devouring mouth, driven half frantic with the powerful sensations of exquisite, almost painful delight.

Anna then moved from her clitoris and ran on the line of Sarah's cunt with the tip of her tongue, then gathered it as it were into a rod and penetrate deep within her labia lips.

"Anna! Anna! I'm going to spend! I'm go . . ing to spend! To spend! I tell you! Oh. . h . . h . . h . . h!" Sarah's voice left her as she inundated Anna's face, but Anna continued her actions, until at last she rose up, her cheeks red with passion, and her bosom shining from the moist offerings Sarah's had ejected.

"At his point, the man will proceed to take his pleasure." Anna grinned as she spoke. "With his two knees between yours he will lean over, not upon you, but supporting himself on his elbow. You then take his prick and plant its head justly and neatly between the lips of your cunt. Then you put your arms round his waist, and with a little pressure on his part, in goes his prick. Its hood slips back, and you feel the sweet thing filling the outer vestibule of your cunt. Then he draws back until he is almost out, and again smoothly and gently pushes in again. This time, with an indescribable thrill you'll feel that big head force its way sweetly past the inner, narrow entrance. Mm, that thrill is so delicious." She sighed and slid on top of Sarah.

"Then he draws back again until he is almost out," Anna continued. "But with a more decided sweep he thrusts his powerful swelling prick back in and buries it half way in your cunt. These movements he continues, always drawing almost out, always gaining, by gentle but smoothly repeated thrusts, grinding into you. Presently, and all too quickly, you feel his pendant balls touch you beneath your buttocks. Then they beat more firmly against you, and last of all his belly, which has been touching yours all along, presses into yours. Your cushion feels his, and his last thrust brings your bodies into the most intimate and close contact.

Now the real delight begins. Every stroke, every thrust he gives, is from head to heel of his prick. He gives you long, smooth, deliberate thrusts; every line of those long seven or eight inches tells upon you. As your pleasure increases, so does, his. Presently his agonies of delight begin. All his nerves seem concentrated in the head of his prick, until his sensations are so vivid as almost to take his senses away. Then begin the all too short, as time is concerned, short digs. He shortens his strokes, but quickens them, banging his balls against you with great force. Suddenly he will spend, pouring out the fullest riches of his manly strength. You feel it flowing fast into you, like a torrent, like a powerful artery shooting its blood into you. He presses you as though he would crush you into pulp. He forces his prick in even further than you would think possible, and then it is over. You have been fucked." She smiled.

"Then comes a delightful interval of repose. He lets his body lie all along yours, and he kisses you, and pets you, and calls you all the pretty things he thinks of. But the fuck is at an end, and cannot be repeated until his prick stands again."

"I cannot wait to experience what you have told me," Sarah pulled Anna into a passionate hug. "But now," she pushed their cunts together. Sarah was maddened with an almost supernatural excess of voluptuous feelings that Anna had inspired within her. She twisted and wriggled their clitorises against each other as they both became drenched with their mutual spending until, exhausted, she lay motionless on top of Anna.

Once they had both somewhat recovered their lost breath, Anna raised her head and kissed her cousin. "There, Sarah," she said. "I have not only told you about sex with a man, but have also taught you of the pleasure one girl can take with another. Apparently, extremely well." She grinned. "I must tell you that some women even prefer such delights to those which man can give them."

"Are you suggesting that I may find a sweet cunt even more to my liking than a fine prick?" Sarah grinned after unexpectedly blurted out these words.

"That is entirely possible. Does it shock you that your sexual orientation includes being with a woman?"

"Actually, I find it truly wonderful how an innocent girl like myself could have been so quickly initiated into becoming a lesbian."

"Well, after you have learned what it is to be well fucked by a man you must tell me which you prefer. Of course, in order to accomplish that you will have to return to London with me.

Chapter Four: To The Nunnery

"Ah I now I feel better, Sarah," Anna remarked as she finished her breakfast. "How do you feel this morning? None the worse, I hope, after our delicious tete-a-tete last night?"

"All the better, I think," Sarah replied with a smirk. "Only I feel rather stretched in the thigh joints."

"That comes from want of practice," Anna told her. "Come, Sarah," she said, standing up. "We breakfasted so late that I think neither of us could eat any lunch. Let us go out for a ramble over the fields. We will take some biscuits in our pockets and discuss the future, for I must soon be returning to London."

They sallied forth, having first told Martha that they might not be in again for several hours. "Ah yes, that's right, Miss Anna," the old woman had said while looking at Sarah with beaming face and smiles. "I do believe that if you had not come here, poor Miss Sarah would be sitting indoors now, moping to death."

"Seriously, Anna," Sarah asked as they began their walk. "Am I really going to be able to go with you to London?"

"Absolutely! Why, to leave you here where you can never know a man would be unthinkable. Not only must you come to London, but you should also live with me and join myself and others in our thriving enterprise. I will prove to you that it is downright folly to keep your beauty so hidden from the world when it can be so well turned to profit by using the charms and senses nature has given you." She grinned, slowly shaking her head at Sarah's confused look. "It is through his pursuit of lust that a woman may exert influence over a man."

"Influence?"

"Money, my dear. A man achieves his needs and desires through your willingness to participate, and compensates you handsomely in return."

"Your business provides you with both pleasure for money? Anna, I confess you have me sorely confused."

"Oh Sarah, you are indeed naive. Have you never heard of a brothel?"

Sarah slapped her right hand over her mouth. "Anna," she gasped a she lowered her hand. "Are you telling me you run a house...a house...of ill repute?"

"Oh Sarah," Anna laughed. "And are you telling me you have never heard of hypocrisy? Come, now without being in the least degree uncharitable towards my neighbors, who in public denounce what they call illicit intercourse as sinful and wicked, I tell you it is those same people who privately flock to our establishment. In fact, there are a great number of gentlemen, both married and unmarried, who come to their lovers there at least once a month, if not oftener."

Sarah listened intently as Anna told her how she became the Madame of The Nunnery, calling herself Madame Q. She explained the nature of the women who worked there, and the exclusively of the establishment. Question after question flooded Sarah's mind, but she could not conceal her growing interest, actually excitement, in what she was being told. "Tell me about the type of men who come to The Nunnery," she asked.

"Oh, my dear Sarah, you may have no concerns in that regard. You can be sure that they are men of the world who have an immense amount of discretion. Our clients must be well recommended, or else they would get no invitations, and the recommendations we get come from the highest quarters."

"Are your ladies able to decide who they wish to be with?"

"Indeed, they are. You, as they, will be entirely your own mistress in that respect. We shall introduce gentlemen to you, and it is for you to introduce them or not, as you please, to your charming little cunt."

An involuntary smile adorned Sarah's face. "But there will be so much more that I need to learn." Her eyes twinkled. "Isn't there?"

"You, Sarah, are just the girl to form into a real priestess of Venus," Anna told her. "I will teach you how to fully use the exquisite and sensitive charms you are endowed with, while at the same time thoroughly enjoying them."

Their conversation continued in this delightful manner as they wandered on, chatting and laughing, and picturing all kinds of lovely events, until they at last returned to the house. Anna went upstairs to write a letter to Natalie, her assistant at The Nunnery, while Sarah went into the garden to pick some flowers. They agreed to meet again at tea time.

"DOES NATALIE KNOW I am coming with you, Anna?" Sarah asked anxiously as she reached for her second scone.

"Oh yes. But until she gets my letter, which I just sent to post, she won't know that our snug Nunnery is to have another lovely novice. We shall soon be leaving for London, for I am badly needed. Read this." Anna gave Sarah a letter, evidently written by a lady, from the character of the writing. It ran thus:

'DEAREST ANNA,

When are you coming back? When will you be able to leave your little country cousin to interview the gentlemen we are obliged to tell that they cannot be accommodated until Madame Q has returned? I hope you are not playing fox, and that all this while you are enjoying pleasures with fox hunting squires or other country gentry. What is Sarah like? Has she any penchant for our ways? Have you sounded her? Do you think, supposing she is pretty enough, she could be induced to give up her chance of a single husband for the certainty of a plurality of much more interesting and ever fresh lovers? Unless she is naturally inclined to do so, I don't advocate her joining our fold. But, on the other hand, I encourage you to recruit additional ladies of pleasure. We have been very busy with not a bed unoccupied from one end of the week to the other. If those beds could speak they would tell us some pretty stories. I believe adultery is greatly on the increase, and some of our ladies have several lovers apiece.

Natalie.'

"WELL?" ANNA ASKED AS Sarah handed back the letter to her. "What do you think I told Natalie in my reply today?"

"I suppose you said that you thought I would go with you?"

"Indeed I did, and I said much more. I told her that you were absolutely beautiful from the crown of your head to the soles of your feet, and that your disposition was so amorous, your temperament so ardent, that you would be the very finest possible acquisition. I told her that I had found you in a state of extraordinary simplicity and ignorance, but that the moment I introduced the ways of enlightening knowledge, you had spread out..."

"Enough, enough," Sarah cried out laughingly, putting up her hand to stop Anna's torrent of words. "I am delighted you told Natalie all this, for I do long for those experiences which you have so eloquently described."

"And your longing shall, very soon, be indulged. I promise."

Few people were traveling to London in the first-class compartments, so the cousins had the carriage almost entirely to themselves the whole way and enjoyed pleasant conversation while watching the scenery go by. A handsome carriage and pair driven by a coachman in a splendid livery, and with a footman who took their trunks, met them at the gate. Anna spoke kindly and gently to both of the men, who touched their hats, and seemed glad to see her again. They then drove rapidly through street after street. The noise prevented conversation, which Sarah was glad of, for she preferred to gaze out the window. She was struck with amazement at the huge London, of which she was then seeing but a small portion.

At length they arrived at their destination and drew up in front of a magnificent house. A beautiful young woman named Annette opened the door, and once they were inside, Anna kissed her and then introduced Natalie. "Who's at home, Annette?" Anna asked.

"Miss Natalie is upstairs, miss."

At that moment an elegantly dressed lady came down the stairs, whom Sarah correctly guessed to be Natalie. She immediately went to Anna, and the two women embraced one another with hearty hugs and kisses, pressing their breasts together, first on one side, and then on the other. They only said a few words to one another before they separated, after which Anna introduced Natalie to Sarah.

"It is a pleasure to meet you, Sarah," Natalie said, smiling, and proceeded to give Sarah a kiss. "Come, let me show you to your room where you can relax and refresh before dinner." She took Sarah by the hand and led her upstairs.

On entering her room, Sarah's eyes immediately fell to the bed. It was immense, the largest bed she had ever seen, a four poster of solid mahogany, its posts being of extra strength to support a huge mirror which formed its canopy. "Not only will you have the pleasure of being fucked," Natalie told her. "But you can also enjoy seeing yourself being enjoyed."

The walls were adorned with pictures, some in oils, some in watercolors, some were engravings, and all of a most erotic nature. There were also two chairs, a settee, an ottoman, a small table and chests of drawers, the one opposite the bed having a large mirror strategically placed to fully reflect activities on the bed. The carpet was luxurious, and there was a thick hearth rug in front of the fireplace.

Natalie remained to sit and talk to Sarah, answering her many questions about The Nunnery, until Annette announced that Sarah's bath was ready.

"Then I shall see you at dinner," Natalie said as she rose, then gave Sarah a passionate kiss on the lips before leaving.

Chapter Five: Deflowered

There were four people who sat down to dinner: Anna, Natalie, Sarah, and a very handsome, well dressed gentleman who was introduced as George. While nothing spicy was appropriate for dinner conversation, it was clear to Sarah that Anna had selected George to be the first man for her to enjoy. Innuendo made her blush, and by the time the dessert was served she had become extremely aroused with anticipation.

The meal concluded, all rose to leave when George took Sarah, holding her at arm's length, and looked at her with eager eyes. His two hands under her armpits, he gazed at her as though he had just that one chance of doing so and never would again. "Sarah," he whispered, in a voice husky with excitement. "May I come to your room tonight?"

Her knees about to buckle beneath her, Sarah clasped onto his waist then raised her face and kissed him. "Yes," she whispered.

Annette came to assist Sarah to undress, and when she was naked produced the nightdress that Anna had selected for the occasion. It was of exquisitely fine and absolutely transparent silken material. It had no sleeves, but it fastened around Sarah's throat with a ribbon which ran through eyelet holes. It was open from top to bottom, but fastened by ribbons which were tied just above and again below her breasts. Ribbons also held the garment in place across her waist, and more loosely at her knees. Its utility as an article of clothing was nil, but it greatly added to the attractiveness of Sarah's charms by veiling them.

Sarah had no sooner donned this elegant costume when a there was a knock at the door, which Annette opened to permit Anna and George to enter. Annette then wished all goodnight and left.

"Come, Sarah," Anna began. "I want George to assure himself, before me, that I deliver you a perfect maiden into his hands."

George put his arm around Sarah's waist and urged her towards the settee. Anna stood before them. "Now, first of all, George, you must let me show Sarah the cock you wish to introduce to her cunt."

"Why, certainly," George laughed.

Anna with rapid fingers undid his waistcoat, and his braces before and behind before unbuttoning his trousers. Then, pulling up his shirt, she produced his magnificent prick. "There!" Anna cried as she placed Sarah's hand around to the delicious hot, hard weapon. "Is it not grand, Sarah? Is it not as delicious to feel as I told you it would be? Now, put your hand in and take out the bag of jewels."

Sarah looked at George, who bent his head forward, and as their mouths met, she took his balls in her hand. A splendid, full, hard, big pair of them, which she could feel slide from side to side as she gently pressed them. George held her a little more firmly and pressed his hand and finger onto her bushy mound. Then, pushing his tongue deep into her mouth, he slipped his middle finger between the full, soft lips of a cunt which, except for Anna's fingers, had been virgin until this time.

"And now has she not a delicious little cunt, George?" Anna asked.

"Awfully nice," was the answer, as his finger gently and sweetly worked up and down. "A perfect little cunt."

When Sarah heard the door close, she realized that Anna had left the room. With a bound George jumped up, and after a quick rustling of clothes he was perfectly naked. How different he was from the slender softness of Anna. George's muscles seemed like engines of great force, as every movement of his made them play under his white and even skin. But what naturally attracted Sarah's most eager attention was that magnificent prick of his.

George noticed her admiration and he gave her time to enjoy viewing his body, but then when he thought she had seen enough for the present he took her hands and stood her up. His hands swiftly untied the ribbons, opening her garment in the front, following which he began to massage her breasts, his head leaning forward to enable him to lick and suck her nipples.

Sarah responded by entwining her fingers in his hair, increasing her grip on his head as her open mouthed panting increased. From nowhere she heard herself say, "Lick me" as she involuntarily pushed his head down. Delighting in the fact he complied, however, she parted her legs as his tongue invaded the space between her labia lips. She spent almost instantly.

George stood up again, his face glistening with her moisture. To Sarah's astonished vision his cock appeared to have grown even longer, bigger, and more rigid than ever. He moved behind her, slipped her nightdress from her shoulders, and half turned her into a deep mouthed kiss as it floated to the ground.

Sarah's hand sought out his rigid rod, and grasping onto it, said, "Take me to bed."

George picked her up and carried her to the bed, kissing her all the way. He gently laid her down, and in a moment George was between the thighs she eagerly spread wide apart for him. He positioned his member and she felt with a thrill the soft-feeling yet powerful bulbous head separate the lips of her throbbing little cunt. The ease with which it penetrated astonished her, for it was almost instantly inside her. She could feel it expanding and filling her as far as it had gone. But George, instead of trying to push it in any further, kept pushing his prick in and out, tickling her in so ravishing a manner that she held her breath to enjoy it the more. All of her feelings seemed concentrated at that one spot. Little throbs began to shoot all about it, and she knew she was at the point of coming. She expected at any moment that George would pump deeper in, but he still continued his play when she suddenly spent.

George had apparently waited for this, for the moment he perceived it he grasped Sarah to himself tighter than ever. Suddenly something rent inside her, an extraordinary sensation of neither pain nor pleasure followed, and with alternate movements backwards and forwards she felt George's prick rapidly gaining ground. For the first time, Sarah knew the infinite joy of being filled and stretched to the utmost by the power of a man.

"Ah! Ah! Ah!" cried George at each stroke, his breath hot on her neck. His balls touched her, and he was all in. He then commenced with splendidly long strokes.

Sarah's arousal deprived her of speech, so only her moans and the writing of her body could convey her delight. The chief pleasure was feeling the alternating filling and contraction of her cunt, which, after a few strokes from end to end, began to grow more and more brilliant, until it seemed to her that she should pass out from the excessive pleasure. There were perfect spasms, like electric shocks in their force and rapidity, which with all the most deliciously soothing sensations proved to her that fucking was, indeed, indescribably delicious.

But alas, even the longest fuck is always too short. George's time was come. All of a sudden, he commenced rapid, short digs which sent Sarah wild with an agony of delight. All the room seemed to whirl round and round. She felt that in another moment she must faint, when, crushing her to himself, George for the last time dashed his prick in to its very furthest limit. Sarah felt as if a powerful pump were sending streams in jets against her inside, which caused her to enter into a half-swoon of ecstasy, a kind of dream in which she was lifted out of all connections to the earth.

It was Anna's laughing voice which recalled Sarah to earth, and looking up she found herself still in George's arms. "Take your head out of the way, George," Anna said to him. "And let me kiss my girl."

Sarah did not know at what precise moment Anna had returned to the room, for once George had begun to fuck her she had no senses to see or hear anything else. Anna had been avidly watching the proceedings, however. Perhaps from the very beginning. "Well, Sarah?" She asked, kissing and petting her.

Sarah, still unable to formulate words, could only smile a response. Anna had taught her what pleasure one girl can give another, but her caresses, ardent as they were, paled before the glory of those which a man could give.

ACCORDING TO NATALIE, Sarah subsequently developed into an extremely fine acquisition for The Nunnery. She specialized in taking her pleasure by dominating both men and women.

THE END

About the Author

With keen interest in nineteenth and early twentieth century history, Dorian Shellan writes a variety of stories with Victorian settings.

The Victorian era was one of great innovations, industrial, medical, and social. Dorian's stories incorporate many of these changes and the impact it had on the population of that time.

Dorian's genres range from novels, including adventure and romance, to short stories, to Victorian erotica.

Read more at https://victorianstories.com.